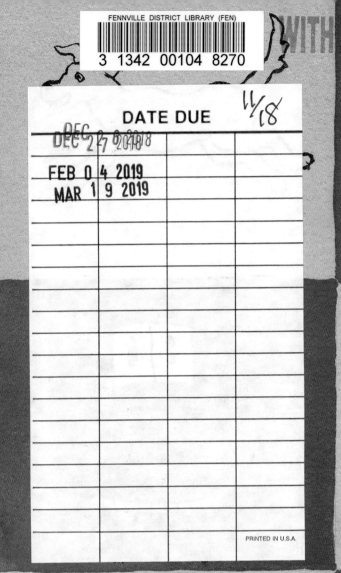

I'M TOUGH!

KATE & JIM McMULLAN

BALZER + BRAY
An Imprint of HarperCollins Publishers

Balzer + Bray is an imprint of HarperCollins Publishers.

I'm Tough!
Text copyright © 2018 by Kate McMullan
Illustrations copyright © 2018 by Jim McMullan
Library of Congress Control Number: 2017955857
ISBN 978-0-06-244925-2

Typography by Andrea Vandergrift
18 19 20 21 22 SCP 10 9 8 7 6 5 4 3 2 1
❖
First Edition

For Arthur Abramson & Lily Abramson

We're grateful to John Worden of Sag Harbor, NY, Ted Chapman of Fort Worth, TX,
and Keith Stapleton of Brooklyn, NY, who talked us through pickup basics.

Thanks to our outstanding HarperCollins crew: Alessandra Balzer, Kelsey Murphy,
Dana Fritts, Andrea Vandergrift, and Kathryn Silsand.

And a truckload of thanks to Holly McGhee, the toughest agent around.

I'm not the
BIGGEST TRUCK
in the parking lot,

but I'm big enough,
'cause guess what—

I'M TOUGH!

Got a CAB up front,
CARGO BED behind.

My TAILGATE?
Drops down flat for
loadin' FREIGHT.

Load #1?

LUMBER!

All ABOOOOAAAAAARD!

RATCHET STRAPS?

Buckle up tight!

My
FANNY FLAG'S
wavin' to say
LOOK OUT!

Got an

EXTRA-LONG LOAD today.

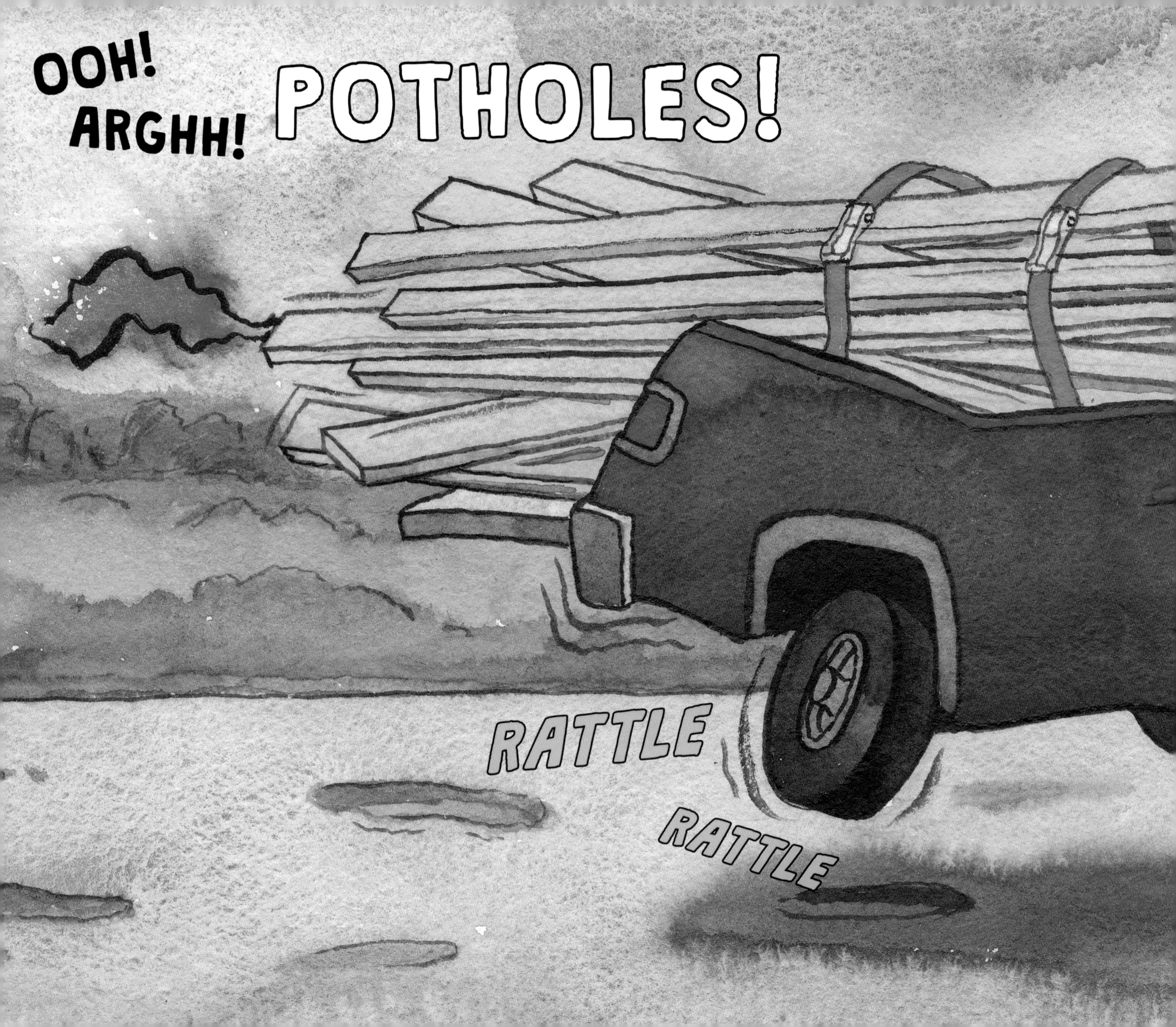
OOH!
ARGHH!
POTHOLES!
RATTLE
RATTLE

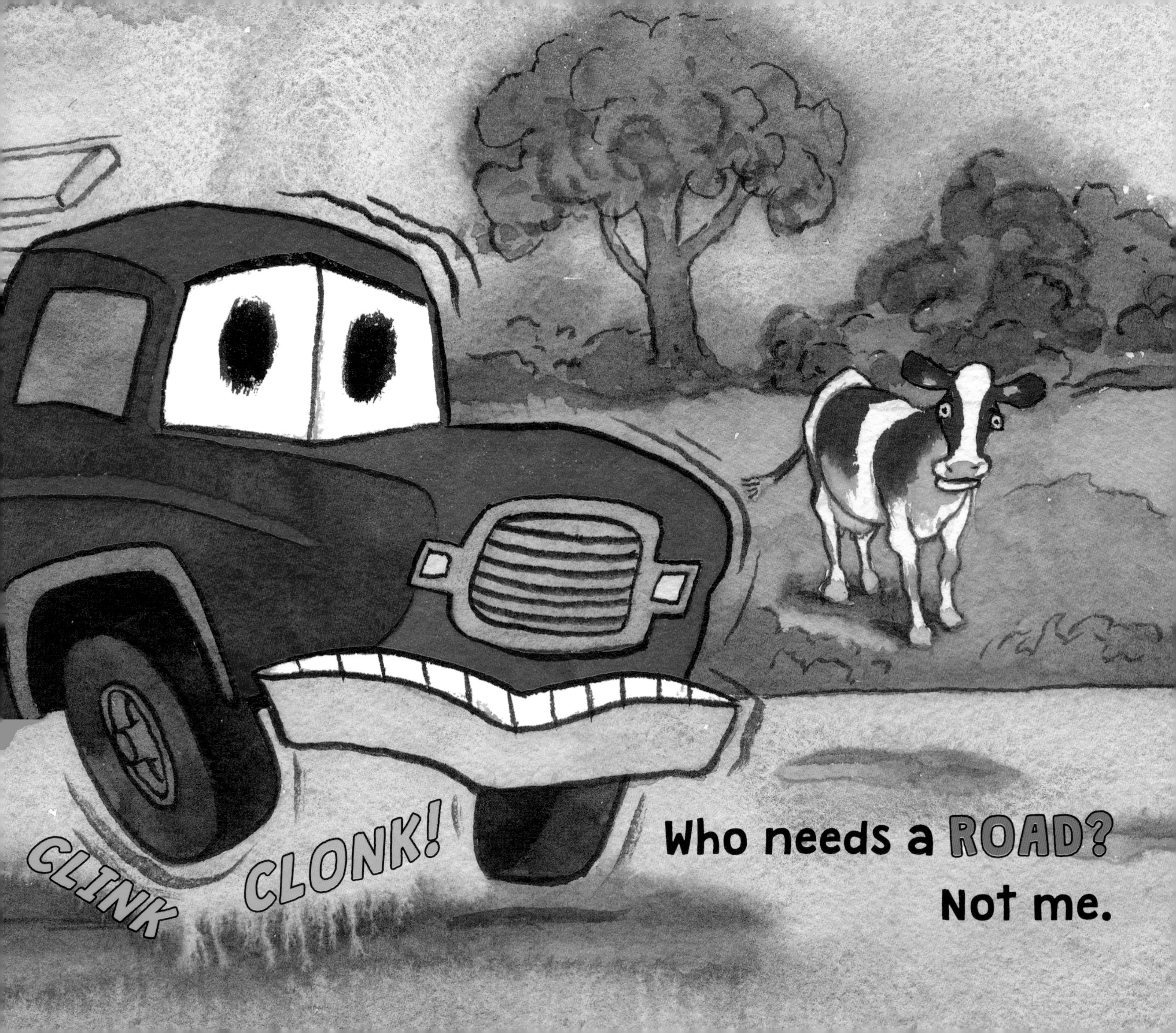

Who needs a **ROAD?**

Not me.

That stretch was ROUGH,
but did I give up? NO!

I'm good to GO, 'cause, you know . . .
I'M TOUGH!

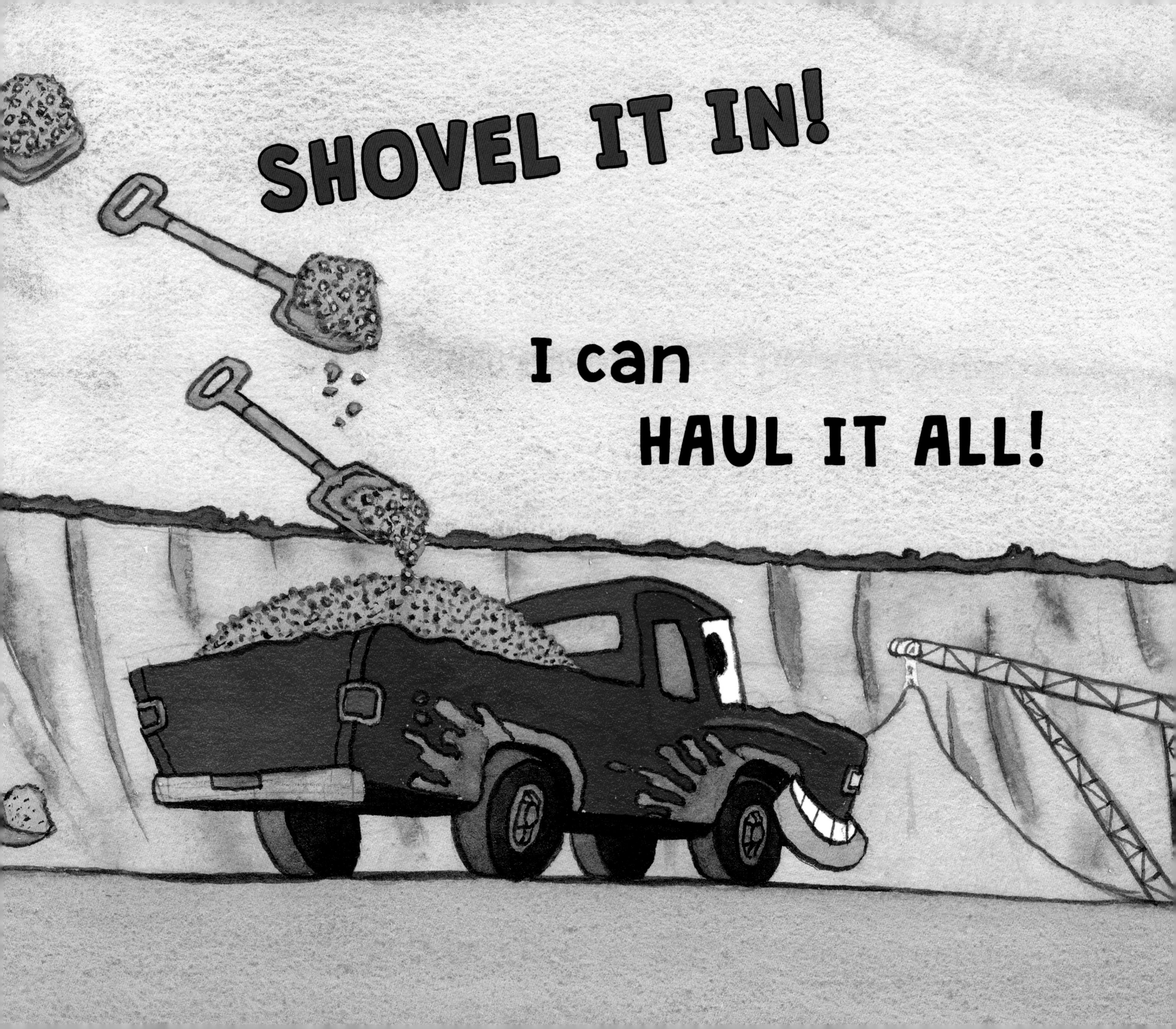

SHOVEL IT IN!

I can
HAUL IT ALL!

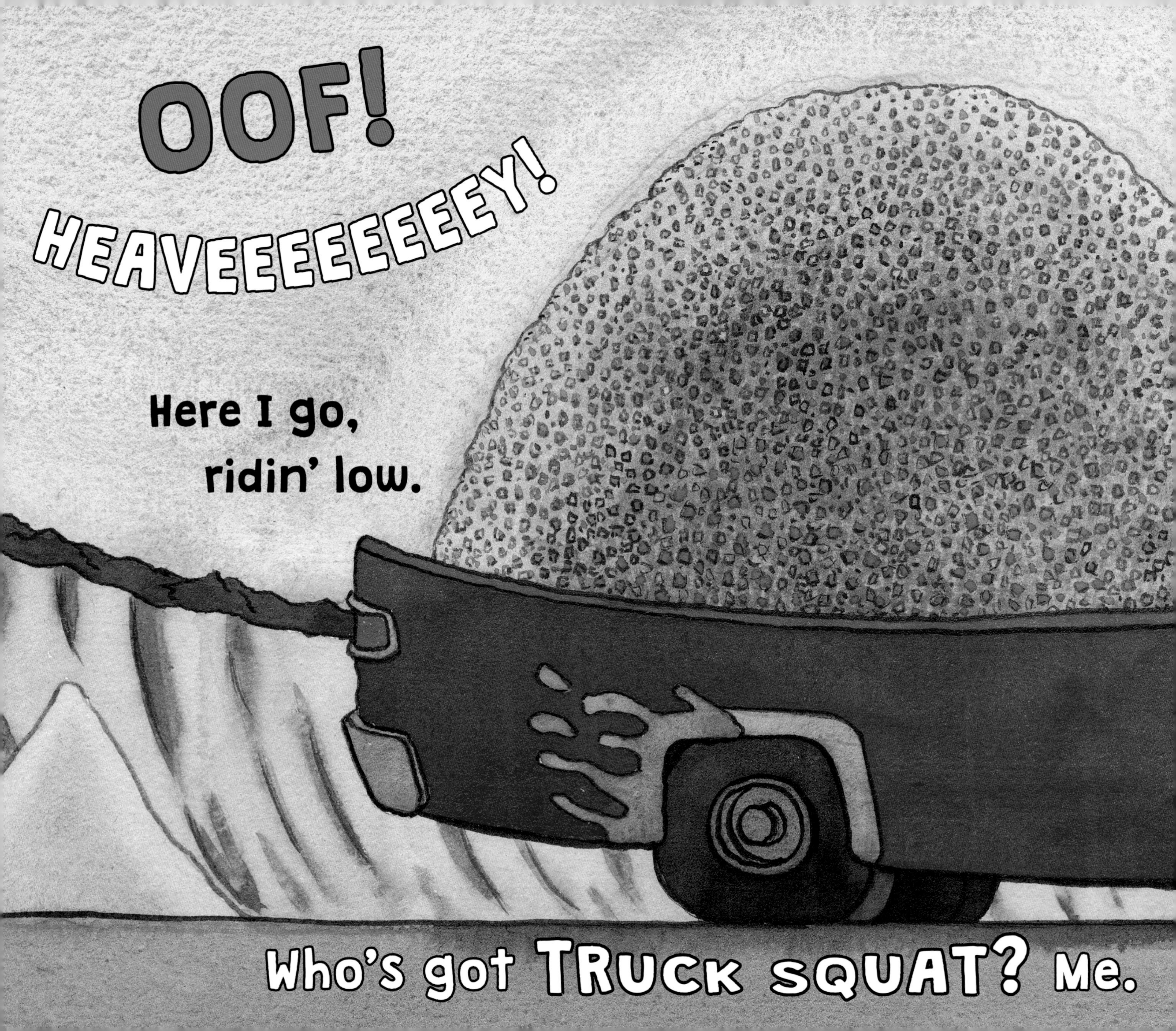

Here I go,
ridin' low.

Who's got TRUCK SQUAT? Me.

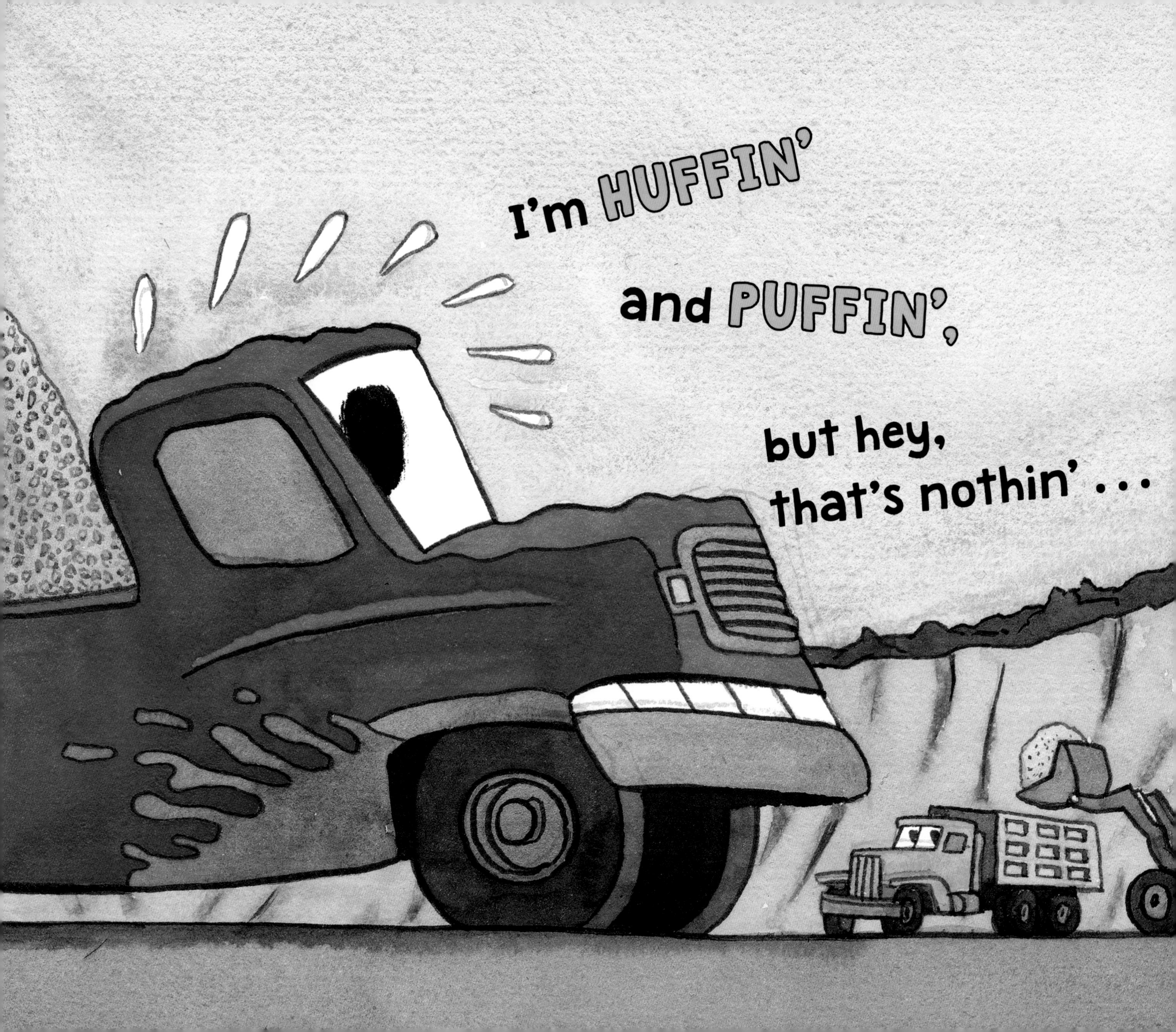

I'm HUFFIN'

and PUFFIN',

but hey,
that's nothin' . . .

'cause when goin'
gets **TOUGH—**

SHIFT it into **4-WHEEL,**
JUMP the **CLUTCH—**

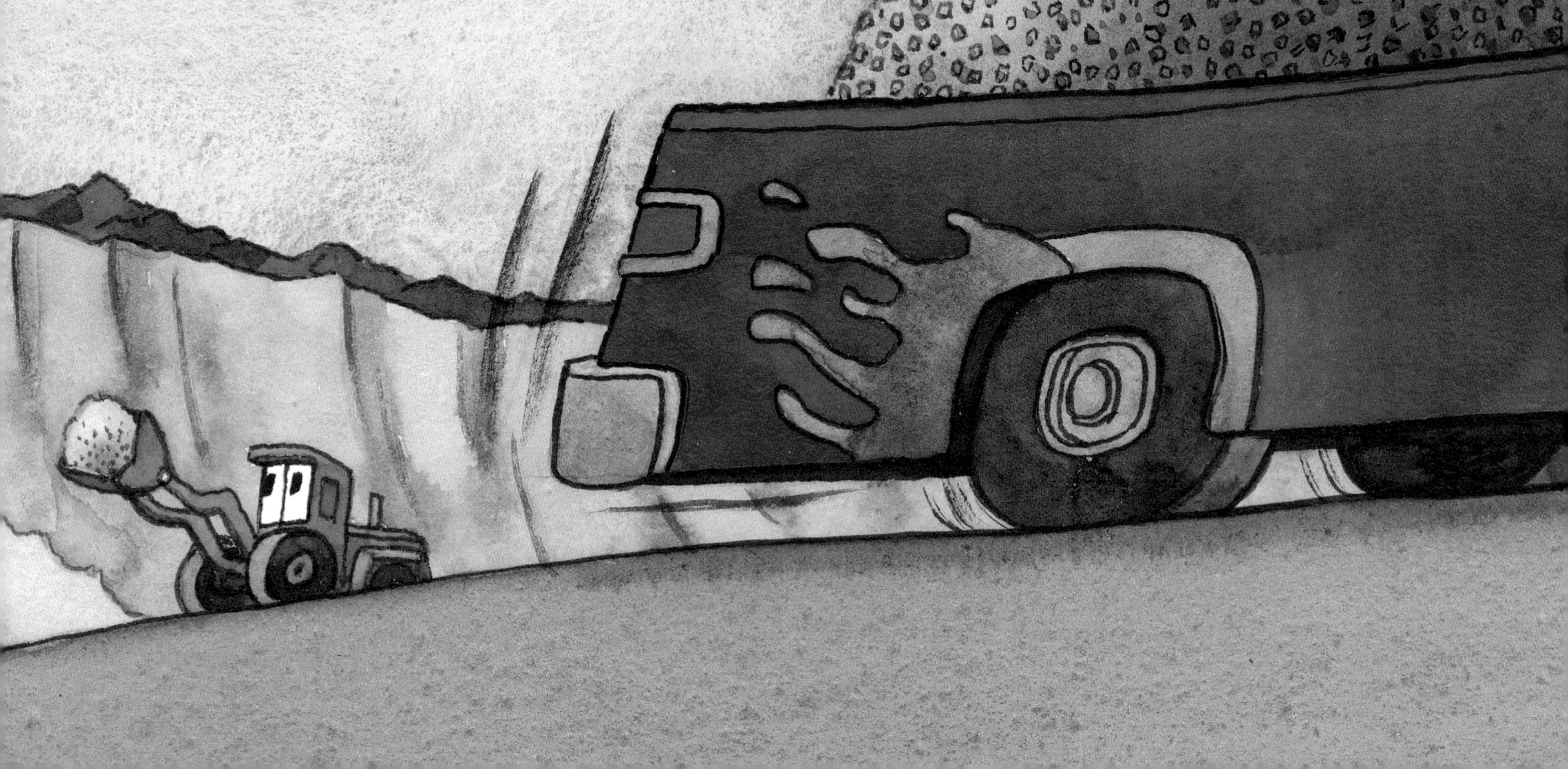

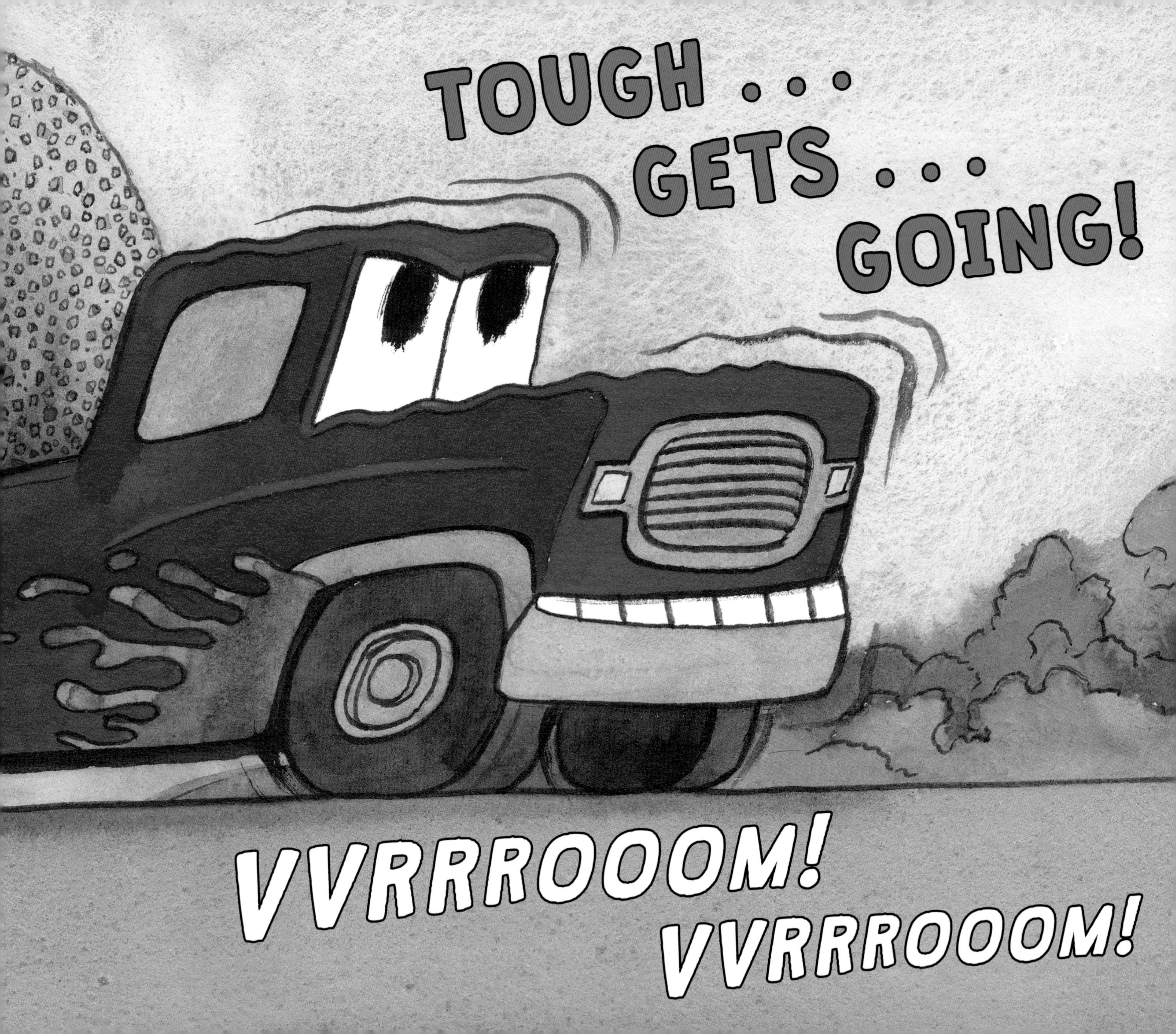
TOUGH . . .
GETS . . .
GOING!
VVRRROOOM!
VVRRROOOM!

Did I TRAVEL
with the GRAVEL?

You KNOW I did!

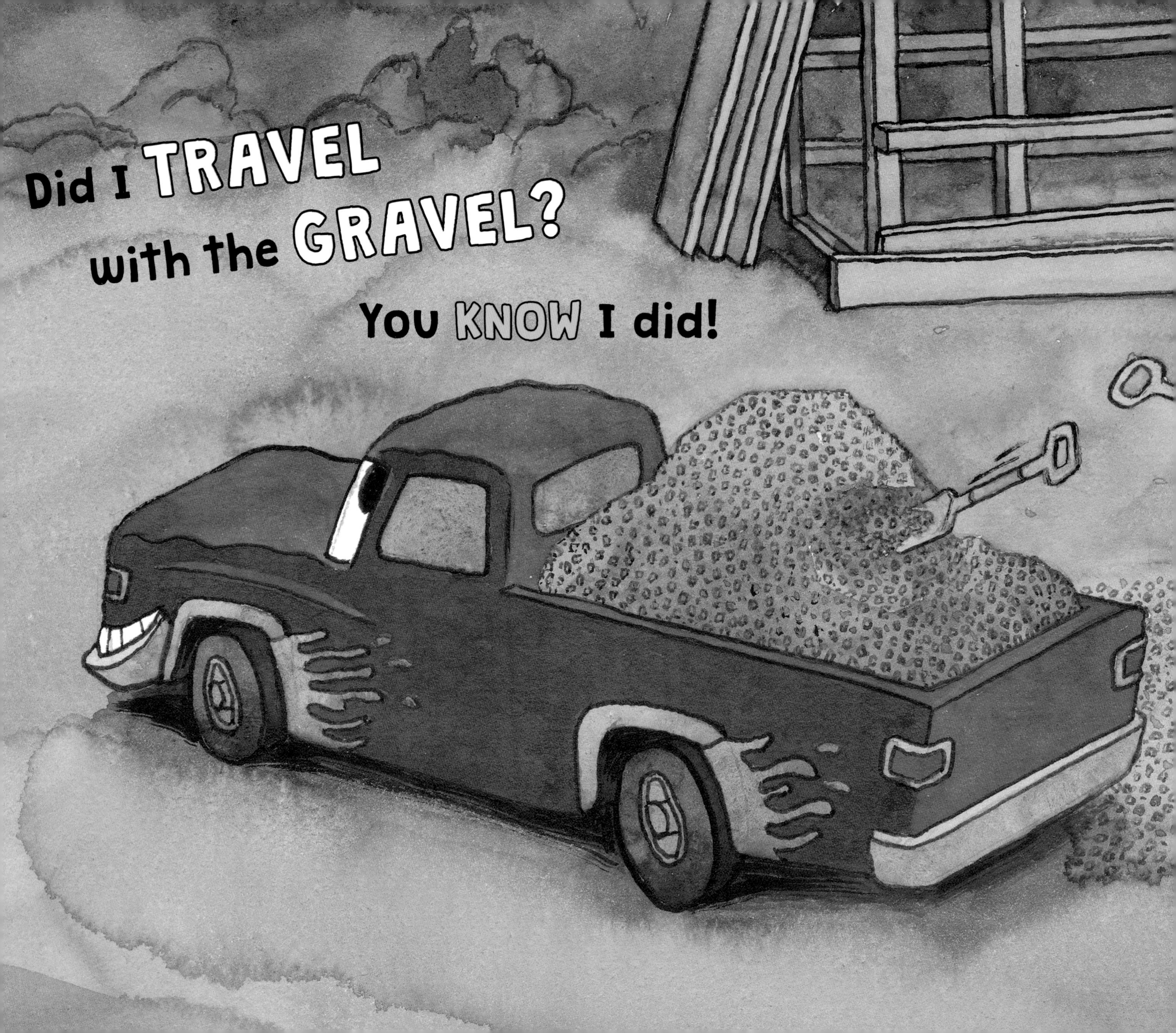

Load #3?

HAY RIDE!

STACK 'em!

PACK 'em!

Tie 'em
with a ROPE!

WHOA!

WHOA!

What a **WHOPPER** of a **LOAD!**

And I gotta drive it on a

CURVY, SWERVY ROAD!

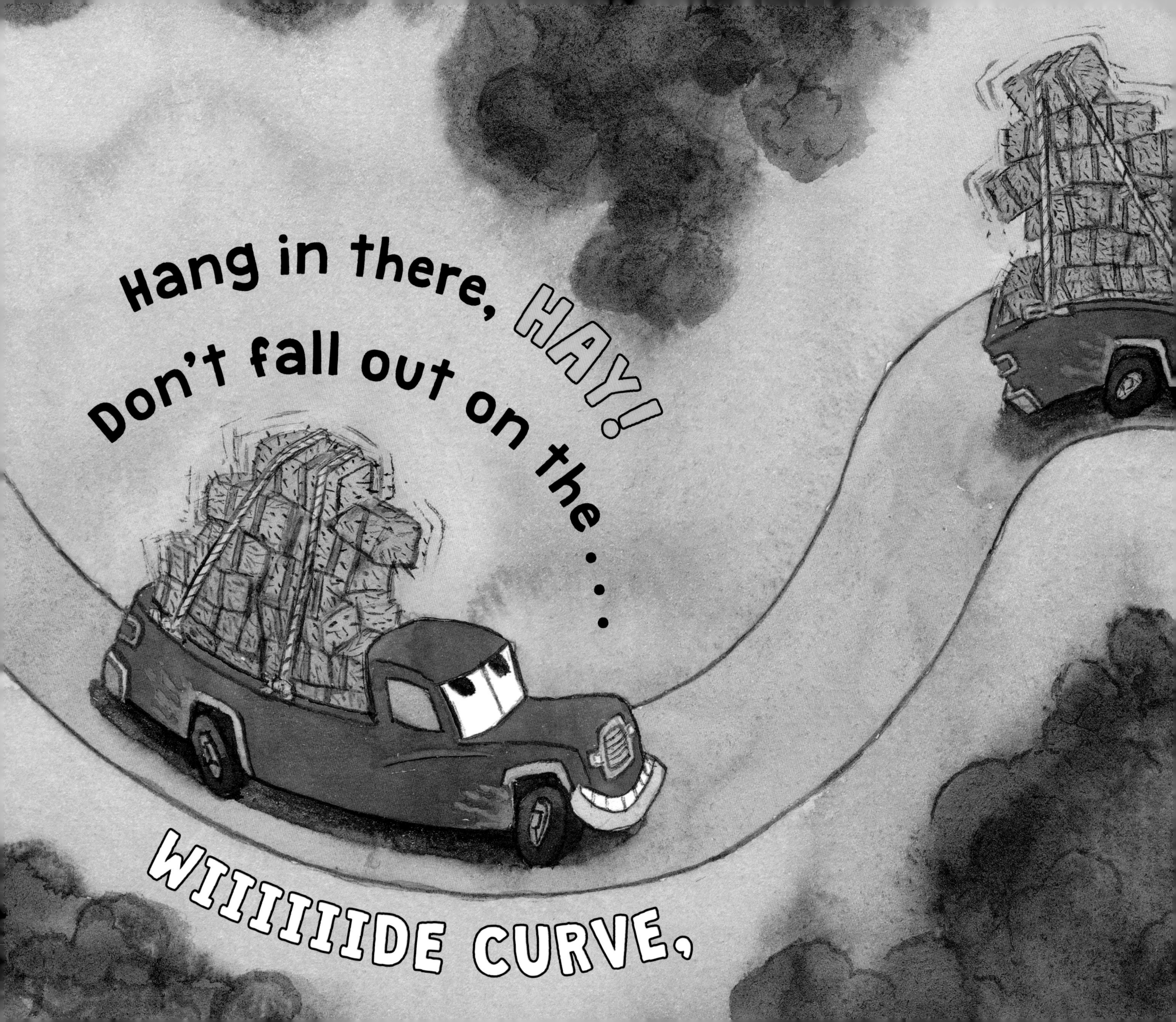

Hang in there, HAY!
Don't fall out on the . . .

WIIIIIIDE CURVE,

HEY, HAY!

Take it AWAY!

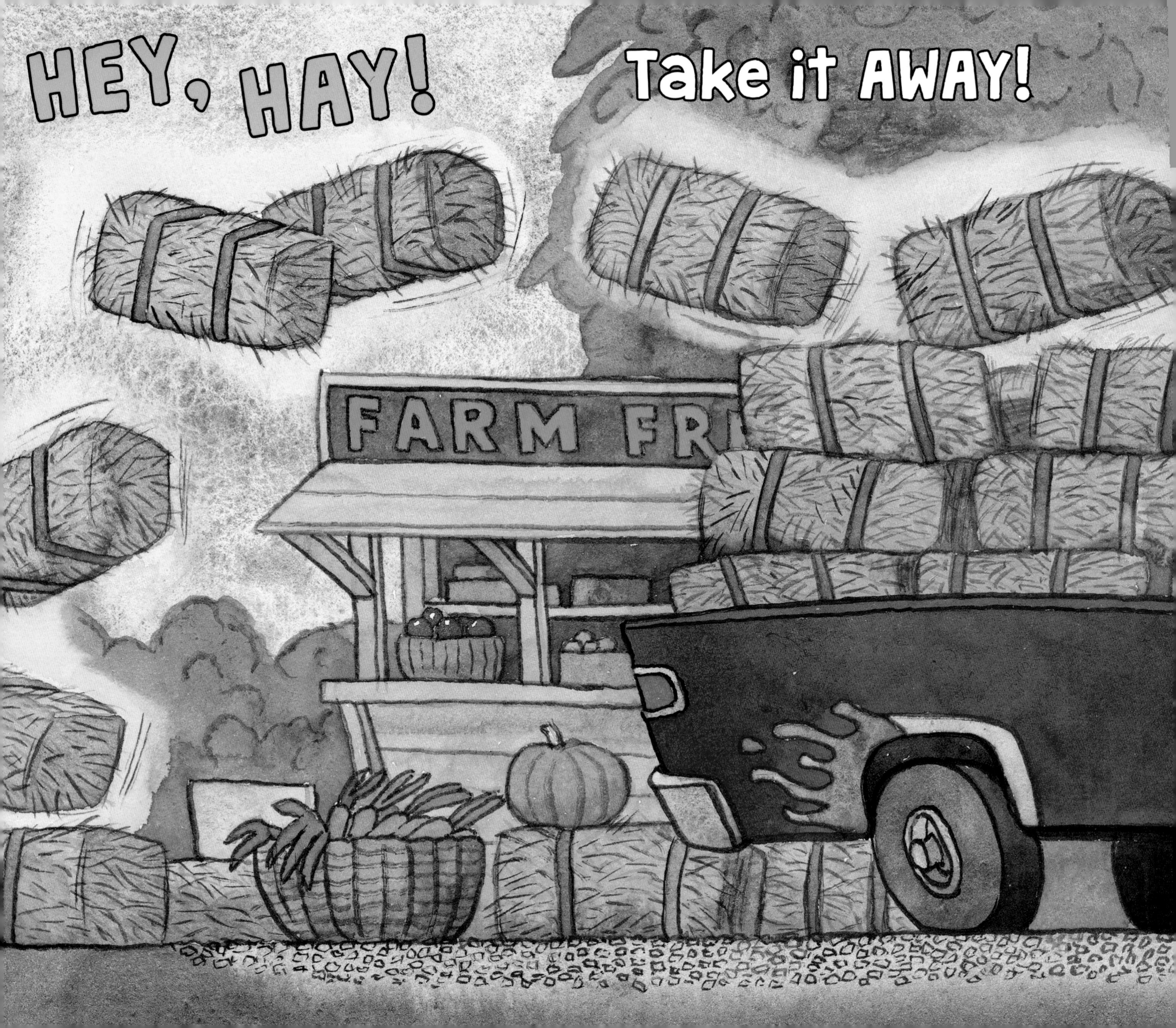

What kinda **LOADS** did I haul today?

LONG LOAD!

HEAVY LOAD!

WHOPPER!

Got the job done,
hauled all the stuff.

PUMPKINS $2

Who am I?
You know—